Every DOG Needs a Boy

Ramona Lusch Johnson

EVERY DOG NEEDS A BOY
Copyright © 2023 by Ramona Lusch Johnson

Scripture quotations are taken from the Holy Bible, New Living Translation, copyright © 1996, 2004, 2015 by Tyndale House Foundation. Used by permission of Tyndale House Publishers, Inc., Carol Stream, Illinois 60188. All rights reserved.

ISBN: 978-1-4866-2398-3
eBook ISBN: 978-1-4866-2399-0

Word Alive Press
119 De Baets Street Winnipeg, MB R2J 3R9
www.wordalivepress.ca

WORD ALIVE
—PRESS—

Cataloguing and Publication information may be obtained through Library and Archives Canada.

DEDICATION

This book is dedicated to my great-nephews and nieces, the children of Armin and Mandy Johnson of Whitehorse, Yukon: Elan (age eleven), Bode (age eight), Heidi (age seven), and Lana (age five). They are an inspiration when it comes to their diligence in the routine of caring for their sled dogs. All four mushers (drivers) were winners in the "sprint" category of the 2023 North American Championship Races held in North Pole, Alaska on March 2–4.

Elan placed first with his team of three dogs. Bode came in third with a two-dog team. Heidi finished first with one dog, and Lana was third in the same category.

These honours, plus some in other locations, are the result of hard work. The siblings have the responsibility of feeding, cleaning up, and wintertime bedding, which is the process of making sure the dogs have dry straw to lie upon. They also must practice with their dogs, training them to obey commands. Kindness with firmness is necessary in forming a winning team.

The Johnson Yukoners and their parents look forward to attending other competitions in Western Canada and Alaska. Happy sledding!

"Where am I?" whimpered a very frightened puppy. He had been sound asleep when he was taken from his home and left in a box beside the road.

When the pup awoke, he stood and peeked over the top of the box. Nothing looked familiar. Red, orange, and yellow leaves lay on the ground around him. He noticed some dry dog food and a bowl of water nearby.

The poor little fellow didn't know his name—if he even had one. He did remember a man's voice calling him "the runt of the litter."

"I will leave him by the side of the road," the man had said. "Perhaps someone will pick him up. We already have too many dogs!"

Puppy's little heart felt sad when he realized that he was not wanted or loved.

He knew his mother loved him, but where was she?

As he pondered his fate, he heard a car pull over and stop. Two children jumped out and ran towards him.

"He's mine!" said the boy.

"He is not!" his sister yelled.

"I saw him first!"

"Did not!"

"Did too!"

They argued as they fought over him.

"If you two brats don't stop your bickering, I will turn around and take that mutt right back to where we found him!" their mother said.

When they got to their home, things were no better. Everyone seemed so angry.

Puppy was scared. At his first chance, when no one was looking, he sneaked away and sped down the road as fast as his short legs would carry him!

Oops! Up ahead was an old shack with a grumpy-looking man standing outside.

"Get out of here, you mongrel!" he shouted as he threw a big boot at the fleeing pup.

Luckily, it missed and flew right over Puppy's head! He ran even faster, and then off the road where he hid behind some tall grass.

Puppy sat quietly, peering out from his hiding place.

He heard the pleasant sound of laughter and whistling. Soon two boys carrying fishing poles came into view, and walking proudly alongside each boy was a dog. They were heading toward the river. All four seemed so happy.

I wish I had a boy, Puppy thought. He wanted so much to join them, but he was afraid. *They might not want me.*

8

A sudden surprise awaited him. A pretty lady named Miss Carol was out for an evening walk when she spotted him. She reached down and gently patted his head.

"Oh you dear little fellow," she said. "You must be lost. You are so cute. You look like a little cupcake. That's what I will call you—Cupcake! I would love to take you to my home. Will you come?"

Puppy didn't know if he could trust this human. His luck had not been good so far, but this lady did seem very kind.

He nodded, but he did not like the idea of being called "Cupcake."

Why would she call me that? he wondered.

As they entered Miss Carol's cozy home, she said, "The first thing I will do is give you a bath."

Puppy didn't know what a bath was. When he found out, he wasn't at all pleased, but afterward he felt much better.

"Are you hungry?" she asked as she placed a bowl of warm milk and some canned tuna before him. The tuna was served on a pretty china saucer. He hurriedly gulped the food down.

The lady continued to fuss over him, making his bed from satin pillows. The bed was soft and very comfortable, and his tummy was full.

A very tired puppy soon fell asleep and dreamed. In his dream, he saw himself walking with the dogs and their boys, whom he had seen earlier in the day.

Puppy had been with Miss Carol for several months. During that time, he grew stronger and taller. Miss Carol had treated him very well, but some things she did annoyed him.

I'm embarrassed when she puts ribbons and bows in my hair, he thought. *I don't like wearing the fancy dog sweaters she puts on me to go walking. She thinks I look cute. I don't want to be cute. Handsome, but not cute.*

As he thought about the things he did not like, Puppy realized that none of them were important. He was beginning to understand Miss Carol's actions better. The reason she had clipped bows to his hair and dressed him in pretty sweaters was that she wanted him to feel special!

By her acts of kindness, she had become very special to him. He was a lucky dog! Miss Carol saw to it that he had fun. She often took the time to play fetch with him. Puppy loved to hear her laughter when he tumbled and rolled in his effort to catch the ball.

Pup gazed up at her fondly. The look in his eyes said what was in his heart: *Thank you for rescuing me when I was lost and had no home. I'm thankful it was you who found me and not those two angry children! I was afraid they were looking for me.*

Miss Carol understood. She knew that such a young pup needed time to learn new things.

One lesson Puppy learned early was about something that Carol called "house training." At first he was puzzled as to why she had placed newspaper on the floor beside the door. It made no sense to him. She knew he couldn't read!

Only after a few unpleasant accidents did he get the message. He was being house-trained!

You have been so gentle and patient with me, even when I didn't behave well, he thought. *You have taught me what love is about.*

"And you, my young friend," Carol whispered, squeezing his paw, "you are as sweet as a cupcake."

At last he understood why she had called him Cupcake. It was a compliment, although only a nickname. Somehow Puppy knew the day would come when he would be given a proper name.

Months later, Miss Carol was surprised to receive an important job offer. She wanted to accept it, but if she did it would mean having to move far away—and worse, she could not take her dog with her.

She was troubled. What should she do? How could she ever part with him?

Suddenly, a name came to her mind. Jimmy! Jimmy was only twelve years old but very reliable. He was kind, loved the outdoors, and fishing was his favourite pastime. Besides this, the boy didn't have a dog. She invited him to come and discuss the matter.

Carol informed the lad that she was searching for a reliable person to care for her puppy and she felt he was the perfect choice. Would he be willing?

"Me?" he asked. "That would make me the happiest boy in the world! I loved your puppy the moment I saw him. I have prayed for a dog like this for a long time."

Puppy couldn't speak like a human, but he understood. He gave two happy barks, which in dog language meant, "Yeah, okay!" He even turned a few cartwheels!

All three agreed on the plan.

Finally, Miss Carol was packed and ready to move. She had tears in her eyes as she whispered, "My sweet little Cupcake, I will always love you."

Her grateful pet smiled a big doggy smile. It was his way of saying, *Now I have two people who I love and who love me—you and my new friend Jimmy.*

Jimmy picked Puppy up and held him close. "You and I will be pals," he said. "A pal is a buddy or a very close friend. Since that is what we are, from now on your name will be Pal."

Puppy barked, "I have a name. I love it! I love it!"

Suddenly, all was quiet. An overly-excited dog became calm and very serious. "Are prayers answered? Do dreams ever come true?" he questioned. He heard that Jimmy prayed for a dog and that he, Pal, was the answer to that prayer. It was Jimmy who has given him the name he loved. He also remembered the very first night he had spent at Miss Carol's. The young dog recalled the dream he had as he slept peacefully and safely in her home. In that dream, he had seen himself walking proudly with two other dogs and their boys. A positive "Yes!" was the answer Pal received to his questions! He looked forward to adventures with his buddy, Jimmy.

If you travel to the river on a weekend, you will probably see not two but three boys. With them will be three dogs. Can you guess who the two newcomers are? You are right! Every dog had a boy!

You care for people and animals alike, O Lord.

How precious is your unfailing love, O God!

(Psalm 36:6)